W9-BYT-310

THE SMURFS
AND THE
MAGIC
EGG

by Peyo

Ready-to-Read

Simon Spotlight
New York London Toronto Sydney New Delhi

SIMON SPOTLIGHT
An imprint of Simon & Schuster Children's Publishing Division
1230 Avenue of the Americas, New York, New York 10020
© Peyo - 2014 - Licensed through Lafig Belgium - www.smurf.com. All Rights Reserved.
Originally published in French in 2009 as *L' oeuf et les Schtroumpfs* written by Peyo.
English language translation © 2014 by Peyo. All rights reserved.
All rights reserved, including the right of reproduction in whole or in part in any form.
SIMON SPOTLIGHT, READY-TO-READ, and colophon are registered trademarks of Simon & Schuster, Inc.
For information about special discounts for bulk purchases, please contact
Simon & Schuster Special Sales at 1-866-506-1949 or business@simonandschuster.com.
The Simon & Schuster Speakers Bureau can bring authors to your live event.
For more information or to book an event contact the Simon & Schuster Speakers Bureau at
1-866-248-3049 or visit our website at www.simonspeakers.com.
Manufactured in the United States of America 1213 LAK
First Edition
2 4 6 8 10 9 7 5 3 1
ISBN 978-1-4424-9570-8 (pbk)
ISBN 978-1-4424-9571-5 (hc)

Grouchy Smurf and Jokey Smurf
were taking a walk in the forest.
Suddenly they stopped.
In the middle of the forest
was an egg!

"Where could this egg have smurfed from?" cried Jokey Smurf. "From a chicken, of course," Grouchy Smurf said grouchily.

"But there are no chickens
in the forest," Jokey said.
"Where do you think it came from?"
"Who cares?" Grouchy asked.

The Smurfs carried the egg
to the village.
Papa Smurf was very surprised
they had found it in the forest.

"Smurf me a spoon," Papa said.
"I am going to break the shell."
He gave the egg a gentle tap
with a spoon. Nothing happened.

He tapped harder.
Still, nothing happened.
Then he gave the egg a strong whack.

The egg did not break,
but the spoon did!
"Let me help, Papa,"
offered Hefty Smurf.

Hefty Smurf tried to crack the egg
with his ax.
Nothing happened.
He swung the ax harder.
Nothing happened.

"Well, turn me into a sausage
if that shell doesn't smurf
this time," Hefty said.

He slammed the ax down
with all his might.
Nothing happened . . . to the egg,
but Hefty turned into a sausage!

"Hefty said, 'Turn me into a sausage,'
and he hit the egg,"
Papa Smurf said.
"The egg granted his wish.
It must be magic!"
The Smurfs looked at one another.
Then they all ran to the egg.

They touched the egg
and made wishes.
"I want a cake!" one Smurf said.
"I want to be yellow!"
another Smurf yelled.
"Make me red!" cheered another.

Smurf Village had never looked
so colorful!
There were yellow Smurfs, red Smurfs,
and even striped Smurfs!
"I like chickens! I like eggs!"
sang a happy Smurf.

Who was so happy? It was Grouchy!
One of the other Smurfs
wished he would be happy,
and so he was!
The Smurfs made more and more
wishes.

"I'd better smurf some order around here," Papa Smurf said. He was about to do something when POOF! Papa was a plain Smurf.

Someone had wished that Papa would
not be Papa Smurf anymore!
Papa spotted a Smurf
with a white beard and red cap.
"Who are you?" cried the real Papa.
"I am Papa Smurf!" said the other.

Things were getting out of control.
Two Smurfs were fighting.
One wished that the other
would become very hairy.

The hairy Smurf wished the other
would have a moustache.
"I must stop this now!"
the real Papa Smurf said.

"I wish that everything would return to the way it was before."
Just like that, the real Papa Smurf had a white beard again.

All the rainbow Smurfs
were blue again.
"Hooray, I'm not a sausage anymore!"
Hefty Smurf said.
"Good! I hate sausage!"
said Grouchy Smurf, grouchy once
again.

But not all the Smurfs were happy.
They ran to the egg with more wishes.
Then they heard a sound:
"Peep! Peep!"

The egg cracked open
and a little chick came out.
"This egg cannot smurf
any more trouble," Papa said.
Everyone walked away
except one Smurf.
He stared at the chick, thinking.

"A chick will become a chicken,"
the Smurf said.
"The chicken will smurf eggs.
The chick came from a magic egg,
so its eggs will be magic too!"

He asked Papa Smurf
if he could have the chick.
"Of course," said Papa Smurf.

The Smurf led the chick away
from Smurf Village.
He built a pen to keep
the chick safe.

Taking care of the chick was hard.
The Smurf had to fetch water
and food for it every day.
And he had to clean the pen.

At night the Smurf was very tired
from caring for the chick.
It took up all his time.
He stopped going to Smurf Village.

A few weeks later he finally
showed up in the village.
He looked very upset.
Papa Smurf asked what was wrong.
"It's my chick. It's terrible!"
the Smurf said.

"Oh no, is the little chick sick?"
Papa Smurf asked.

"Not at all, Papa!
It's very healthy.
But after all this time, and all my
smurfy work . . .
really, it's just not fair."

Papa Smurf followed him to the pen.
He peeked in and quickly
saw what had happened.
This bird would never smurf
a magic egg.
Only hens lay eggs,
and the chick had grown up . . .
into a rooster!